C000294814

797,885 Books

are available to read at

www.ForgottenBooks.com

---◆---

Forgotten Books' App
Available for mobile, tablet & eReader

ISBN 978-1-334-68468-5
PIBN 10745041

This book is a reproduction of an important historical work. Forgotten Books uses
state-of-the-art technology to digitally reconstruct the work, preserving the original format
whilst repairing imperfections present in the aged copy. In rare cases, an imperfection in
the original, such as a blemish or missing page, may be replicated in our edition. We do,
however, repair the vast majority of imperfections successfully; any imperfections that
remain are intentionally left to preserve the state of such historical works.

Forgotten Books is a registered trademark of FB &c Ltd.
Copyright © 2017 FB &c Ltd.
FB &c Ltd, Dalton House, 60 Windsor Avenue, London, SW19 2RR.
Company number 08720141. Registered in England and Wales.

For support please visit www.forgottenbooks.com

1 MONTH OF
FREE
READING

at
www.ForgottenBooks.com

By purchasing this book you are eligible for one month membership to ForgottenBooks.com, giving you unlimited access to our entire collection of over 700,000 titles via our web site and mobile apps.

To claim your free month visit:
www.forgottenbooks.com/free745041

* Offer is valid for 45 days from date of purchase. Terms and conditions apply.

English
Français
Deutsche
Italiano
Español
Português

www.forgottenbooks.com

Mythology Photography **Fiction**
Fishing Christianity **Art** Cooking
Essays Buddhism Freemasonry
Medicine **Biology** Music **Ancient**
Egypt Evolution Carpentry Physics
Dance Geology **Mathematics** Fitness
Shakespeare **Folklore** Yoga Marketing
Confidence Immortality Biographies
Poetry **Psychology** Witchcraft
Electronics Chemistry History **Law**
Accounting **Philosophy** Anthropology
Alchemy Drama Quantum Mechanics
Atheism Sexual Health **Ancient History**
Entrepreneurship Languages Sport
Paleontology Needlework Islam
Metaphysics Investment Archaeology
Parenting Statistics Criminology
Motivational

"Paradise Flats,"

A Comedy in Three Acts,

—BY—

HUBBARD TAYLOR-SMITH,

AUTHOR OF

"The Lottery Ticket;" "New Year's Reception."

COPYRIGHT, 1889,

—BY—

HUBBARD TAYLOR-SMITH.

All Rights Reserved.

BYRON S. ADAMS, PRINTER.

"Paradise Flats,"

A Comedy in Three Acts,

—BY—

HUBBARD TAYLOR-SMITH

AUTHOR OF

"The Lottery Ticket;" "New Year's Reception."

COPYRIGHT, 1889,

—BY—

HUBBARD TAYLOR-SMITH.

All Rights Reserved.

◆─►

WASHINGTON, D. C.
BYRON S ADAMS, PRINTER,
514 EIGHT STREET.

13236

CHARACTERS.

Miss JANE MEREDITH, a spinster.

FANNIE MEREDITH, Miss Jane's niece.

CLARA BOSWELL, } Fannie's friends.
SUSIE JONES,

Mr. LARRY SINGLETON, an old batchelor.

HERBERT SINGLETON, Mr Larry's nephew, in love with
    Fannie.

CHARLIE STACEY, in love with Susie.

ROB BENNINGS, in love with Clara.

CHINA, presiding angel of Paradise Flats.

Scenery.—Hallway and Parlor of Paradise Flats.

Time.—The Present.

TMP96-006757

PARADISE FLATS.

ACT I.

SCENE.—*Parlor and Hallway of Paradise Flats. Curtain rises discovering China setting room to rights. She is singing a plantation melody.*

CHINA. Deed and deed, dem young gemmen is gitting wusser and wusser ebery day of deir libes. Young Mister Herbert is not so bad, but Mister Charlie and Mr. Rob, dey is the debbil's own chillum to muss tings up. No matter how nice I fixes dis yar house, dem young men is not in de place five minutes before it looks like it was struck by a cycloone, an' I darsent say a word. But law sukes, I can't stan' here talkin all day. Miss Jane Meredith's comin' hyar with de young ladies dis afternoon, fer to dine, and Mr. Herbert told me if dere was a speck ob dust or dirt about de place as big as a pin point, dere would be blud on de moon, an' it wouldnt be hisn. Lan', lan', lan', talk about woman's work a nebber gittin' done. Heres nearly four o'clock, Mister Herbert's white wescott to iron, and Mister Rob's collar to do ober, not enough starch iu it, and de up stairs to dust, and lan' knows what, besides watchin' de dinner. (*Takes an umbrella and a pair of overshoes from top of piano and holds them up.*) Now, just look at dat. Some of Mister Rob's doin'. (*Carries them out into the hall and puts umbrella in stand and shoes along side the hat rack.*)

(*Enter Rob from street door, overcoat, hat and gloves on.*)

ROB. For heaven's sake, China, haven't you finished cleaning up. You are slower than the seven year itch. (*Throws gloves on sofa.*) The fellows will all be in in a minute (*puts hat on piano*), and we hav'n't any time to spare. (*Looks at watch.*)

Four fifteen, just an hour and three-quarters in which to dress and get ready for the folks. Did those flowers come? (*Throws overcoat on chair.*)

CHINA. Yaas, sir.

ROB. Well, I'm going up to dress. Tell the fellows to shake it up when they come. *Tempus fugit,* and so do I. (*Exit thro' hall and up stairs, singing, as he goes.*)

CHINA. (*Pouncing on hat, coat and gloves.*) Now just look at that, and den blowin' me up for bein' slow and callin' me a seven year itch. Deed dis nigger's life is a hard one. (*Carries things out to hat rack and hangs them up, putting gloves in pocket of overcoat.*)

(*Enter Charlie from street; hat, overcoat and gloves on.*)

CHARLIE. Holy smoke! Woman, I left you this morning at 9 o'clock cleaning up and here you are still at it, at half-past four. (*Throws overcoat on table in parlor, cane on sofa, and hat on piano.*) You are getting lazy. Any of the fellows in?

CHINA. Mister Rob has just dun come in.

CHARLIE. (*Calling.*) Ah there! Robbie, me boy?

ROB (*Up stairs, calling.*) Stay there, Charlie, me che-ile.

CHARLIE. Well, I've got to hustle to get ready for the folks. Tell Mr. Herbert, when he comes in, that he will have to stir his stumps. (*Exit through hall and up stairs.*)

CHINA. (*Looks despairingly at coat, hat, and gloves for an instant, and then viciously pounces on them and carries them to hat rack as before.*)

(*Enter Herbert in great hurry, overcoat, hat and gloves on; looks at watch.*)

HERBERT. Great guns; a quarter to five and the folks coming at six. (*Throws hat, overcoat, gloves and cane anywhere and everywhere.*) Just my confounded luck. Always have to dress in a hurry. (*Commences to undress as he leaves the room and continues until he has reached the top of the stairs and disappeared.*)

CHINA. Dats de business end of de cycloone. (*Picks up*

things as before and carries them to hall.) Dem young gemmen will kill dis nigger yet.

ROB. (*Coming to head of stairs in shirt sleeves, drying his face on a towel.*) China, where the devil is my high collar? You promised to have it ironed and in my room by the time I got home.

CHINA. I'll do it right away Mister Rob. It will only take me a minute, sir, an'—

CHARLIE. (*Appearing at head of stairs, minus coat and vest.*) China, where is my white wescott?

CHINA. I'se gwine to do it right away, Mr. Charlie, an—

HERBERT. (*Calling from over banisters.*) China, where the Sam Hill are my clean shirts?

CHINA. Dey's in your bureau draw.

ROB.
CHARLIE.   } There's blud on the moon, nigger, an' it aint
HERBERT.   } ourn.

(*Exit up stairs.*)

CHINA. (*Scornfully.*) Blud on de moon is dere. *Yaas,* dere'll be *asnic* in your soup some of dese days if you don't stop worritin me. (*Ring at door bell. China starts for door.*)

ROB. (*From head of stairs.*) China? If that's a bill for me, I've gone out of town and won't be back again for a year.

CHINA. Yaas, sir.

CHARLIE. (*From head of stairs*) China, nobody is at home. You understand.

CHINA. Yaas, sir.

HERBERT. (*From top of stairs*) China, if that's the butter-man tell him we had to chain his last lot to the table.

CHINA. Yaas, sir. (*Ring at door bell*) Yaas I'se comin. Better pull dat bell hanel off an' be done with it. (*Opens door discovering Mr. Larry Singleton, valise in hand.*)

CHINA. (*Taking him for a pedler*) Don't want no Sapolio, silver polish, sewin' machine provements, books, or knife sharpeners. Don't want nuffin (*starts to shut door*).

UNCLE LARRY. Hold on, hold on, woman. What do you take me for?

CHINA. Whose you calling woman, man? What you want? You book agents is so sassy.

UNCLE LARRY. (*Laughing*) Book agent. Lord bless us, that's a good one on me. I'm no book agent.

CHINA. Well, you'se a sewin machine man, an' dats wuss.

UNCLE LARRY. Well, I should say so. But, my dusky princess, I'm neither the one nor the other. Is this the domicile known as Paradise Flats?

CHINA. It are.

UNCLE LARRY. It are, eh. And does Mr. Herbert Singleton live here?

CHINA. He do.

UNCLE LARRY. And is that gentleman at home?

CHINA. Who is you?

UNCLE LARRY. Why do you ask?

CHINA. Cos' if you'se a man with a bill, he is out of town for a year.

UNCLE LARRY. Oh! ho! I see. Well I don't happen to be a man with a bill. I am Mr. Herbert's Uncle Larry, and if you have no objections I wish you would inform him of the fact that I am about the premises. So fly, Queen Kapiolani and do me bidding.

CHINA. (*Goes to hall door and locks it.*) Dat uncle business *may* be all right, but if dem overcoats is gone when I comes back dar'll be blood on de moon for shuah. (*Puts key in her pocket and exits up stairs.*)

UNCLE LARRY. (*Looking around as he takes off his gloves.*) So this is Paradise Flats. Well, I must confess it is not such a misnomer after all. The boys have shown decidedly good taste in fitting up the place, but I suspect some fair hands had the general management of arranging things. This little parlor looks as dainty as a young lady's boudoir. All the more so after my lonely life in the mining districts.

(*Enter* Herbert, *hastily, hands outstretched in welcome. He is in full dress*).

HERBERT. Why my dear Uncle Larry. This *is* a jolly surprise.

(*Shakes hands cordially*).

UNCLE LARRY. Can this be my nephew Herbert?

HERBERT. Well, it just is. Remember it has been fifteen years since you saw me and I guess I've changed a *little* in that time.

UNCLE LARRY. (*Still holding* Herbert's *hands.*) Well, well, it beats all. Let me get a good look at you. (*Takes him by the sholders and looks him over.*) Yes, yes, it is you. You have your mother's eyes and mouth and the same soft brown hair. Dear me. Who would have thought of you having grown up in such a short time, from a little freckle face rascal of ten into a handsome young man, and yet fifteen years is a *long* time. Didn't you expect me, my boy?

HERBERT. Oh yes, of course, I received your letter, but you named no definite time and although we were on the lookout for you, we didn't expect you until next week.

UNCLE LARRY. But what is the meaning of all this gorgeousness, swallow tail and all?

HERBERT. Oh yes, of course. In the pleasure of seeing you it quite slipped my mind. You are just in time. You see Fannie Meredith, Susie Jones and Clara Boswell, three very particular friends of ours, have been crazy to get a glimpse of the interior of Paradise Flats, and to gratify them we give a little dinner party in their honor, and they are coming this evening at six, (*Uncle Larry makes a grab for his valise*). Here, here, none of that, my respected Uncle.

UNCLE LARRY. (*Expostulating.*) Yes, my dear boy, but—

HERBERT. (*Taking valise away from him.*) Don't "dear boy" me. The very idea.

UNCLE LARRY. But Bert, I'm not prepared to meet any ladies, I'm—

HERBERT. Nonsense. You'll just even up our party. You can take care of the chaperone, Miss Jane Meredith.

UNCLE LARRY. Miss Jane Meredith?

HERBERT. Yes, Fannie's aunt, you know, she's coming to play propriety.

UNCLE LARRY. You don't mean Cy. Meredith's sister?

HERBERT. The very same. Why, look here, Uncle Larry, it seems to me I remember something about your having been spoons on her when you were a youngster. By George, how jolly, you wont be a stranger at all. The girls all know you. They ought to. I've spouted Uncle Larry until they know you from a to izzard. Here come the fellows, I'll just make you acquainted, then rush you up stairs where you can tidy up a bit and by that time the folks will have come. (*Enter Rob. and Charlie.*) Uncle Larry, I want you to know my chums, Charlie Stacey and Rob. Bennings, two of Heaven's own children. Fellows, this is the Uncle Larry you have heard me speak of so often. (*Uncle Larry shakes hands cordially with Rob. and Charlie.*)

UNCLE LARRY. Glad to know you, young men. Herbert's friends are all mine.

ROB. Ah! we know you quite well, Uncle Larry—I really beg your pardon—Mr. Singleton, I mean. Bert. you are responsible for *that* slip.

UNCLE LARRY. Let it be Uncle Larry, my boy. Birds of a feather flock together, and if you are chums of my boy, I am quite willing to Uncle you both.

CHARLIE. And we are more than willing to be adopted by any of Bert's relatives, Mr. Singleton.

HERERT. Well, Uncle Larry, I don't want to hurry you, but you won't have any too much time to dress before dinner So come along (*picks up valise, starts into hall and up stairs, Uncle Larry following.*)

ROB. (*Throwing himself on sofa.*) So that is " Uncle Larry." Fine looking old chappie, ain't he?

CHARLIE. Yes, and has a barrel of money they say. Struck it rich in the mines.

ROB. (*Mournfully*) I wish I could strike it rich somewhere.

CHARLIE. So do I, but there's precious little prospect, unless we hit the Louisiana State Lottery. Got a ticket this month?

ROB. Oh, yes, as usual. Why! last month I built a house, bought a brougham and pair, set up a tiger in livery and all on the prospect of getting the capital prize.

CHARLIE. And your ticket drew—

ROB. As usual, a blank. But I had lots of fun building air castles all the same, so I don't begrudge the money.

CHARLIE. (*Looking at watch.*) Quarter of, just time to blow a cloud. Have one (*offers Rob a cigarette which he takes and lights*).

ROB. I thought you had sworn off.

CHARLIE. Now that's funny. I was just about to make the same remark regarding you. (*They look at each other for an instant and then laugh.*)

CHARLIE. Well we won't count this once. But I say, Rob, what made *you* swear off. Dosen't Miss Clara like cigarette smoke?

ROB. (*Innocently.*) Miss Clara who?

CHARLIE. Oh bless his innocent heart. Why Clara Boswell of course.

ROB. I'd like to know what she has to do with my smoking.

CHARLIE. You would, my precious innocent. Well, I got it from pretty good authority that you and the fair Clara were thinking seriously of surprising your friends by a wedding in the near future, and if that is so, Miss Clara may be acountable for a good many little changes for the better in your habits of late.

ROB. (*Brusquely.*) The devil she may. I wish to goodness people would leave me and my affairs alone. Confound it. A fellow can't look at a girl now-a-days, but that all the long-tongued busy bodies commence to make arrangements for an early wedding.

CHARLIE. Then it is not true that you are engaged to her.

ROB. Stuff. As much truth in the assertion that—

CHARLIE. What?

ROB. That you are engaged to Susie Brown. (*Charlie starts.*

Aside.) I guess I hit home that time.

CHARLIE. You don't mean to insinuate that people say that of me.

ROB. I certainly do, and what is more, you have given them plenty of grounds for doing so. Oh, you needn't look so black. You danced every other set with her at the Gushington's blow out last week, and every time she danced with some body else, you stood off in a corner to yourself and sulked.

CHARLIE. The deuce I did. (*Aside.*) By Jove, I must be more careful in the future.

ROB. Well, I suppose congratulations are in order.

CHARLIE. Congratulations be hanged. I wish people would stop talking of my affairs and attend to their own, confound them.

ROB. Then you deny the soft impeachment.

CHARLIE. Of course I do.

ROB. Then we are even. But say, now that we have *confided* in each other, what do you think of Herbert's little affair with Fannie Meredith?

CHARLIE. I don't know, I'm a little bit suspicious of that couple. He's awfully gone on her, and if one can judge from the embroidered slippers, mantel covers, handkerchief cases, umbrella holders, etc., etc., that adorn his room, somebody is very much spoons on him, and that somebody is—

ROB. Fannie Meredith, of course, for he won't look at another girl. He is a sly dog and will bear watching, but—hush— here he comes. (*Enter Uncle Larry and Herbert.*)

UNCLE LARRY. (*Talking as he enters.*) Well, whoever thought of it conceived a most brilliant idea. The house is a perfect little gem. (*To Rob and Charlie*) I have just been telling Bert, how much I admire your quarters. Why they are dainty enough for the most exacting young lady. And Herbert tells me that the entire place, house, furnishing, and everything, falls to the one who marries first. A capital idea. Just the place for a young married couple. I'm afraid two of you will have to move pretty soon, Eh boys?

HERBERT. Oh, bless you, no. We are all confirmed bachelors.

ROB. Yes, I, for one, am too desperately fond of the fair sex to ever think of setting my young affections on any particular one member.

CHARLIE. And I, too fond of bachelor freedom.

UNCLE LARRY. And I, too, am a confirmed old bach. What do you boys say to taking me in as a permanent member of your family.

ALL. You!

UNCLE LARRY. Why not. I'm not as old as I look, and I haven't forgotten my youthful days. After fifteen years of hard work I would like to settle down and enjoy myself, for a time at least. I'll promise to conform to your rules and regulations, and if you boys will agree to put up with a grumpy old customer like myself, just say the word, I'll buy a quarter interest, cash down, and become at once a permanent angel myself.

HERBERT. Well, you see, Uncle Larry—we—you haven't forgotten that the house goes to the one who marries first.

UNCLE LARRY. Oh not at all. No danger of my marrying and you all have just said you have no idea of doubling up.

ALL. (*Hesitatingly.*) Oh—yes—yes.

UNCLE LARRY. Very well then, there is nothing to prevent my coming in with you if you'll have me. One more will lighten your expenses, and I will promise not to be a wet blanket. What say you?

HERBERT. Yes, by all means, if Rob and Charlie are willing.

ROB, CHARLIE. More than willing, Mr. Singleton.

UNCLE LARRY. Then it is settled. Herbert, I'll give you a check for my share after dinner. Bless me, I feel ten years younger already. (*Door bell rings.*)

HERBERT. (*Running to window.*) Here they are at last. (*Goes to hall door, which he tries to open.*) What the devil is the matter with the door? (*Tries it again.*) By Jingo, its locked and the key is gone. (*Bell rings.*) China! China! (*Runs into the parlor and hammers on call bell.*) (*Enters China.*)

HERBEBT. How did that door get locked?

CHINA. I locked it, sah.

HERBERT. What the devil did you do that for.

CHINA. Dat man dar said he was your uncle, and I was spicious of him. I wasn't gwine to lebe him with dem overcoats and de front door unlocked. Ugh! ugh, honey. Dere'd be blud on de moon for shuah. (*Bell rings.*)

HERBERT. (*Raging.*) Where's the key, you idiot? I'll discharge you to-morrow.

CHINA. No, sah, honey. You discharges me now, dis minute.

ROB. (*Hurriedly.*) For Heaven's sake, Bert, be careful. We'll be ruined if the woman leaves us in the lurch.

CHINA. Well, I'se gwine to lebe. Dis bery instinct. Here's your ole key. (*Starts to leave room. All the fellows fall on their knees and grab hold of her dress.*)

HERBERT. I beg your pardon, China. I really didn't mean what I said.

ROB. Oh, China; dear, good, sweet China! Don't leave us in the lurch. (*Bell rings.*)

CHARLIE. We'll raise your wages and give you six evenings out if you will only stay.

CHINA. (*Relenting.*) And no more blud on de moon?

ALL. Never!

CHINA. Den I'll stay. Lan' of goodness; I was only funnin'; you couldn't drive me away from de place. (*Opens the front door.*) Howdy, ladies. Walk right in.

(*Enter Fannie, Susie and Clara, followed by Miss Jane. China takes wraps, hangs them up and exits.*)

HERBERT. We thought you were never coming. Have been peeping out the window for the last half hour, and every time a carriage came in sight we thought it was yours. Awfully glad to see you.

ROB. Well, well, so you've gotten here at last. Was afraid you had repented of your bargain and was going back on us; but you are here now, and we intend keeping you as long as possible.

CHARLIE. By Jove. This is jolly. First time the Flats has been honored by the presence of ladies, and I declare it certainly brightens up everything wonderfully.

FANNIE. Oh, my! Isn't this just heavenly. It is just too cute. You know, we have been crazy to come and was awfully afraid Aunt Jane would back out; but we were bound to come anyway, weren't we girls?

SUSIE. Oh this is just gorgeous. Just too awfully too too; and to think of you men living here all by yourselves. Aunt Jane, just think of it. The boys live here just like it was a really true home. It's too awfully jolly.

CLARA. Oh my, we thought that old carriage would never get here, the horses were too poky for any use. You know I could't sleep a wink last night for thinking about all of us coming up to-day.

NOTE.—*The above lines of Herbert, Rob, Stacey, Clara, Susie and Fannie are spoken very rapidly and in a chorus.*

AUNT JANE. (*Raising her hands above her head.*) My! My! My! Such a buzz. You'll make me deaf for two months to come.

UNCLE LARRY. (*Aside.*) The saints preserve me.

FANNIE. (*Starting into parlor, jumps back.*) Goodness! Herbert, who is it?

HERBERT. O, I quite forgot. That's Uncle Larry, just arrived from Colorado; come in, I want to present him. (*They enter the parlor.*) Uncle Larry, let me present you to Miss Fannie Meredith. Fannie, my Uncle Larry Singleton. (*They shake hands.*)

FANNIE. So glad to meet you Mr. Singleton. I know you quite well from hearing Herbert speak of you so often. (*The others come in from hall, Susie and Clara first and Miss Jane last.*)

HERBERT. Young ladies, my Uncle Larry Singleton. Uncle Larry, Miss Susie Jones and Miss Clara Boswell. (*They bow.*) Miss Jane let me present my Uncle Larry Sing—

AUNT JANE. (*Starting.*) Larry—Mr. Singleton.

UNCLE LARRY. (*Starting forward.*) My dear Jane, this is indeed a pleasure.

ALL. What, you know each other?

UNCLE LARRY. Do we know each other? Do you hear that Jane? Do we know each other? Why, youngsters, we knew each other long before you were born.

AUNT JANE. (*Coquetishly.*) Why, Mr. Singleton, don't make me out a regular Madame Methuselah, if you please.

UNCLE LARRY. (*Laughing.*) Well, well; perhaps I did put it a leetle too strong, but it has been a long, long time.

FANNIE. It's just too jolly to think of your knowing each other. Aren't you glad you came Aunt Jane? It is simply gorgeous, the house and every thing.

(*Portiers leading to dining room are thrown aside and* China *enters.*)

CHINA. Dinner is ready, folks.

HERBERT. (*In angry, aside.*) Confound you, nigger. I told you to say " dinner is served, Mr. Singleton."

CHINA. (*Aside.*) Lans sake! More blud on de moon.

HERBERT. (*To company.*) You see we are prompt. Uncle Larry you take Miss Jane, Charlie you and Miss Susie, Rob you and Miss Clara, and Fannie I'll take you out. (*Orchestra plays march and curtain falls quickly as they start for dining room.*)

End of Act I.

ACT II.

SAME SCENE AS BEFORE.—*Curtains over door leading to dining room drawn, showing party at table, finishing dessert. As curtain rises, all are laughing heartily.*

ROB. And the funniest part about it, is that it is true. One of the Club fellows was an eye witness to the whole affair and he says he laughed his sides sore.

HERBERT. (*Rising.*) Well, we'll leave you to Rob's tender mercies if Miss Jane will excuse Fannie and myself. I want to show her some curios Lieut. Hamsden brought me from China. Come Fannie.

FANNIE. You don't mind, Auntie, do you? I'm just frantic to see everything about this lovely place. (Herbert *and* Fannie *come down from dining room and examine bric-a-brac.*)

CLARA. Oh, I want to see them too.

ROB. So you shall, I'll show them to you.

SUSIE. And I want to see them.

CHARLIE. *I'll* take care that *you* see them, Miss Susie.

HERBERT. (*Down front.*) Yes, and here on the mantel is a genuine satsuma vase. (*They go up to the mantel.* Herbert *puts his arm about* Fannie.) Oh you *darling*, I was awfully afraid you was'nt coming.

FANNIE. (*Attempting to escape.*) Don't, Bert.

HERBERT. (*Innocently.*) Don't what?

FANNIE. Don't hug me like a bear.

HERBERT. Well give me a kiss and I'll let you go.

FANNIE. I won't.

HERBERT. (*Coaxingly.*) Please do?

FANNIE. I won't, I tell you; let me go!

HERBERT. Well, I'll take one. (*Struggles with her and finally succeeds in kissing her. She promptly boxes his ears.*)

FANNIE. There! I hope you are satisfied.

HERBERT. (*Ruefully rubbiny his ears.*) I am if you are. (*They both laugh.*)

FANNIE. You mean thing. (*They come down to sofa.*)

HERBERT. Well, what do you think of the house?

FANNIE. It is just *lovely*.

HERBERT. I am glad you like it, and now, dear, this is our chance. There is absolutely nothing to prevent our announcing our engagement and being married at once. The fellows can get their traps out, and we can just step in and take possession on our return from the wedding trip. Come now, dear, what do you say?

FANNIE. Oh Herbert, it is so awfully soon.

HERBERT. Soon? Haven't I been hanging around you for a whole year? Besides we have got to hurry matters or Bob and Charlie will get ahead of us and then good bye to our much talked of plans for house keeping. I'm getting very suspicious of both Stacey and Bennings. Have you tried to pump Susie and Clara?

FANNIE. Indeed I have, and they both crossed their hearts that they were not engaged.

HERBERT. Oh! the little fibbers. I don't believe a word of that, do you?

FANNIE. (*Laughing.*) Not a *syllable*. And then they turned on me and asked me if I was engaged to you.

HERBERT. Yes, and what did you say?

FANNIE. I told them an *awful* fib. I said I couldn't abide you. You know a girl is never expected to tell the truth about her engagement.

HERBERT. (*Laughing*). Of course not. And now, dear, about the day. Shall we say the 30th of this month?

FANNIE. (*Hesitatingly.*) Y-e-s, if you really wish it.

(Susie *and* Charlie *start down from table.*)

HERBERT. Of course I wish it, you little witch. (*Kisses her.* Susie *and* Charlie *see the kiss. They step behind the screen by piano*). By Jove, it will paralyze the fellows when I spring it on them that I will become a benedict on the 30th.

FANNIE. Clara and Susie will *never, never*, speak to me again, I know.

HERBERT. It's agreed then. Let us go into the conservatory. I want to show you some of our new plants. (*They exit into conservatory.* Charlie *and* Susie *emerge from behind screen.*)

SUSIE. Did you ever? The artful minx.

CHARLIE. Ah! ha! I *thought* so. And now, Susie, you see my suspicions are well founded and if we don't hurry up our wedding, we are goners as far as the house is concerned. Now, *do*, like a *dear, sweet, little woman*, settle matters now. Herbert said the 30th, did you hear him, that meant the date they have agreed on for their wedding. Let us fix ours for the 29th. (*They sit on sofa.*)

SUSIE. Oh, dear me, I never could get ready by that time.

CHARLIE. (*Sadly.*) Then it's good bye to the house. Besides what have *you* got to get ready?

SUSIE. Oh, lots of things. There's the bridesmaids to be asked, and you *know* they have got to get *their* things ready, then there's—oh, lots of things.

CHARLIE. Yes, and in the meantime, Herbert and Fannie will announce their engagement and then—the jig is up. Did you pump Clara?

SUSIE. Yes, and she said that she don't care "that" (*snaps her finger*) but she told a story I know.

CHARLIE. Did she try to pump you.

SUSIE. I should say so. I just told her and Fan I wouldn't marry you if you were the last man on earth, but I didn't mean it dear, *indeed* I didn't.

CHARLIE. Of course you didn't, you little goose. (Rob. *and* Clara *come down from table.*) I understand perfectly. (*Kisses her.* Rob. *and* Clara *see the kiss and step behind screen by piano.*) And now do say the 29th. That's one day ahead of Fan. and Herbert.

SUSIE. I suppose I'll have to say yes.

CHARLIE. Oh you darling. It's settled then (*rising*) and I

think we can look on the place as ours. Come down into the kitchen, I want to show you the culinary arrangements.

(*They exit into hallway as* Rob. *and* Clara *emerge from behind the screen.*)

Bob. Ah! Ha! I smell a mice.

Clara. Yes, and a pretty good sized one, I must say. Did you see her kiss him, and the deceitful girl told me only yesterday she fairly loathed him. (*They sit on sofa.*)

Rob. By Jingo, this is rich. The 29th, eh? Well, we see. I tell you, Clara, we've just got to hustle, and that is all there is about it, or get left in the lurch. It will never do to let them get ahead of us. Fan and Herbert have evidently fixed their wedding for the 30th, and Charlie and Susie we overheard agree on the 29th for theirs, so now by fixing ours for the 28th we will get ahead of both. What do you say?

Clara. It's awful sudden, but (*sighing*) I suppose it's got to come some day, and a month or two earlier wont make much difference.

Rob. (*Warmly.*) Well. (*Rises.*) You don't seem very enthusiastic over the subject, Miss Boswell; perhaps you would like to retract your promise altogether.

Clara. Oh, you great goose, you can't stand a bit of teasing.

Rob. (*Eagerly.*) Were you only teasing?

Clara. Of course I was, and to prove it, I'll agree to the 28th of this month, willingly.

Rob. Clara, you are a brick. Jupiter! Won't the fellows howl when I spring it on them. Come here, I want to show you something. (*Goes up to mantle.*)

Clara. (*Following.*) What is it, dear?

Rob. (*Putting arm around her.*) Why, this. (*Kisses her.*)

Clara. You bad boy.

(*Uncle Larry and Aunt Jane come down from the dining room.*)

Miss Jane. (*Looking around.*) Dear me. Where are the rest of the young people?

ROB. Oh, Herbert and Charlie are showing them over the house. Do you want to follow suit, Clara?

CLARA. Yes, indeed.

ROB. Come along then. (*Then exit into dining room.*)

AUNT JANE. I am doubtful as to the propriety of my allowing all of this, my duties as a chaperone——

UNCLE LARRY. Oh, nonsense, Jane; let the youngsters alone. Remember, we once were young.

AUNT JANE. (*Sighing.*) Yes, many, many years ago. Do you know, Mr. Singleton, that you have changed but little?

UNCLE LARRY. Mr. Singleton. I like that. Drop the Mister, if you please, unless—you prefer I should call you Miss Meredith.

MISS JANE. Oh, no. I rather prefer the use of the Christian names, because—well, you know—

UNCLE LARRY. Because what, my dear Jane?

AUNT JANE. (*Softly.*) Because it brings me face to face again with the happy days of our youth.

UNCLE LARRY. Ah, those were happy days, were they not? (*Sighs.*)

AUNT JANE. Happy, indeed. (*A short pause follows, during which the two glance slyly at each other.*)

AUNT JANE. How does it happen that you are still unmarried, Mr. Singleton—I—I mean—Larry?

UNCLE LARRY. I have been too busy since I left Washington—fifteen years ago—to think of such a thing as matrimony. Besides——

AUNT JANE. Besides what?

UNCLE LARRY. Why, besides the fact I could never forget my first love.

AUNT JANE. (*Stiffly.*) You couldn't have been very deeply in love, or you would have never gone away without a farewell word and remained silent all these years without even a sign that you still lived, and all on account of a trivial misunderstanding.

UNCLE LARRY. I didn't go without a farewell word. I

found I was in the wrong and wrote a most abject apology, begging forgiveness and promising never to be jealous again. I also said that unless I was forgiven, I'd never return.

AUNT JANE. (*Rising.*) Larry Singleton. Do you mean to say you sent me a letter on the morning after our quarrel?

UNCLE LARRY. (*Rising.*) Jane Meredith, do you mean to say you never received my letter?

AUNT JANE. (*Earnestly.*) Larry, I swear to you that I never received it.

UNCLE LARRY. And I swear to you, Jane, that I sent it the morning after our quarrel. (*They stand for a second, facing each other.*)

UNCLE LARRY. (*Holding out his arms.*) Jane.

AUNT JANE. (*Rushing into them.*) Larry. (*She sobs on his shoulders while he blows his nose violently to conceal his emotion.*)

UNCLE LARRY. (*Soothingly.*) There, there, dear, don't cry. (*Savagely.*) Oh what infernal asses we've been—I—I—beg pardon, dear, I mean what an infernal ass I've been. Fifteen of the best years of our lives lost all through my pig-headedness. And you never ceased to love me through all that time.

AUNT JANE. (*Wiping her eyes.*) Never. After you left me on that unfortunate evening, vowing never to return, I went to my room and cried as though my heart was breaking, and would have given the world to have recalled my hasty words. But you were absurdly jealous, dear, and tried me sorely.

UNCLE LARRY. I was a brute, dear, a heartless brute. But I am wiser now, and nothing is to be gained by grieving over what is done and gone. Now that I have you again, I don't mean to let you go. Listen, dear, I've come back to you, a battered old scarecrow, compared to what I was when I won your heart fifteen years ago. But my heart is still young, and it has never ceased to beat for you and you alone, and to-day, you are, if possible, dearer to me than ever. Fortune has been kind to me, and I am counted a rich man. Will you not let me share it with you? Perhaps the future holds some happy days in store for us.

AUNT JANE. But, Larry, dear, I've grown old, and gray, and —

UNCLE LARRY. Stuff and nonsense. Neither of us will crack under the wings, my dear, and as far as growing gray is concerned, I love every gray hair in your head. Why, your eyes are as bright and your cheeks as pink as in the olden days, when we as boy and girl lovers used to go hand in hand strolling through the woods. But now to arrange matters. We've lost too much time already, and at our stage of life one precious minute is equal to an hour of fifteen years ago. So, my dear, we'll get married without delay and go to house-keeping at once. Come now, sweetheart, what do you say ?

AUNT JANE. (*Confusedly.*) I—I—pray give me time to think.

UNCLE LARRY. Not an hour, not a blessed minute. I have thought for both of us. To-morrow morning, bright and early, I'll get the license. At two in the afternoon I will call for you, ostensibly to take a drive. We'll go at once to the Presbyterian Parsonage and have the thing over, without fuss and feathers. Is it a go.

AUNT JANE. (*Smiling.*) The same impetuous Larry of old.

UNCLE LARRY. (*Eagerly.*) You consent then.

AUNT JANE. (*Giving him her hand.*) If you wish it, yes.

UNCLE LARRY. Hurray. Give me a buss, dear. (*Kisses her heartily.*) By the great horn spoon, I'm happy. (*Sings in a craked voice,*) "Jane, Jane, me bunnie Jane."

AUNT JANE. For goodness sake Larry, don't. What will the children think ?

UNCLE LARRY. The children be blowed. Excuse me, dear, I can't help it, I must sing or do something or I'll bust. Besides they are all in the same boat. (*Sings.*) "There's nothing half so pleasant as Love's young dream." Oh, by the way. An idea strikes me. A splendid idea. You know the boys, Herbert, Charlie and Rob, when they started bachelor house-keeping, agreed that the first one married was to fall heir to the entire outfit, furniture, pictures, piano, everything.

AUNT JANE. Yes, so I understand, and a capital plan it was, too.

UNCLE LARRY. Well, don't you see?

AUNT JANE. See what?

UNCLE LARRY. I am a member of the Flats. One of the angels. I purchased a quarter interest in the place this afternoon, agreeing to stand by the rules and regulations and—

AUNT JANE. Yes!

UNCLE LARRY. Well, as I am the first to be married, the place comes to me.

AUNT JANE. But, Larry, you really wouldn't think of turning those young men out of this cosy little home?

UNCLE LARRY. Not a bit of it my dear, not a bit of it. But I intend to give them a pretty good scare to-morrow afternoon, when we return from our " wedding tour." We'll call on them on our way home.

AUNT JANE. It will be an awfully good joke, but hush— here they come.

(*Enter Herbert and Fannie, Charlie and Susie, Rob and Clara.*)

FANNIE. Oh, Aunt Jane, you ought to see the lovely flowers in the conservatory.

SUSIE. And the cutest kitchen.

CLARA. And the dearest little butler's pantry.

AUNT JANE. Well! you seem to have been pretty much all over the premises.

ROB. Come, Clara, and give us some music.

UNCLE LARRY. Yes, do, Miss Clara. It's been a long time since I've heard any.

CLARA. Well, if Rob will play my accompaniment.

ROB. With much pleasure. What shall it be?

CHARLIE. Sing * * * * * * (*here is introduced the latest popular waltz song. At the conclusion of song, all applaud.*)

CLARA. And now, Herbert, it's your turn.

HERBERT. All right, something with a chorus, so we can all take a hand.

(*Here follows a medley of popular airs which closes the scene.*)
End of Act II.

ACT III.

SCENE SAME AS 1ST AND 2D. (*Japanese screen in front of mantel at right. Another in front of piano. Portier over door leading to dining room closed. Curtain rises, discovering* China *dusting.*)

CHINA. Fine doins in dis yar house las night. Guess dem young men thinks Ise stun bline and deaf. From de looks of things dar'll be a weddin' in dis yar house mighty soon an' it won't be mine, dats suttin an' shuah. Spose Misto Charlie thinks I didn't see him and Miss Susie when dey was in de pantry. I didn't nuther, but I heard them, (*imitates the sound of kissing.*) Hi, golly, and dars was Misto Rob. and Miss Clara on the back poach, and Misto Herbert and Miss Fannie in dat obserbatory. Well, I'm not sprised at dem. Young folks will be young folks. But I am suttinly sprised at Miss Jane Meredith, sittin in de parlor holding hands with Misto Herbert's Uncle. Oh, I seed 'em when I kum up fum de kitchen to de dinin room and dey can't proobe no aliby by dis chile, dey wuz dar. (*Ring at the door bell.*) Now, who in de name of goodness is comin hyah dis time o'day. It can't be de young men, cos dey is not due till fo o'clock. (*Ring at bell.*) Yaas I'se comin. (*Goes to hall door and opens it, discovering* Fannie *who enters hurriedly.*) Why lan' of goodness, if it aint Miss Fannie. Why howdy, honey.

FANNIE. Oh my! I'm frightened to death, China. Nobody is at home of course.

CHINA. No indeedy! 'cept me.

FANNIE. Mamma and Aunt Jane would just have a fit if they knew I was up here, but Herbert asked me to come and look around and see if there was anything I thought the house needed, and of course I couldn't think of asking anybody to come with me. China, do you think you can keep a secret?

CHINA. Deed I can, honey.

FANNIE. Well, I'm going to marry Mr. Herbert very soon. We are going to come and live here, and, of course we are going to keep you.

CHINA. Deed is you, honey. (*Laughs.*) For de lan's sake.

FANNIE. Yes, but be sure now not to breathe a word. There is a dollar for you. You needn't mind staying, I can look around myself.

CHINA. Thank you, Miss Fannie. (*Going.*) For de lan's sake. (*Exit.*)

FANNIE. I had to tell her why I came up. Now let me see. (*Looks around parlor.*) The parlor will do nicely. (*Meditatively.*) I might move the piano over here and put the blue plush chair there; then one of those screens will have to go into the dining room, and—(*ring at door bell. Fannie gives a slight scream.*) Oh dear! somebody's coming and I'm caught. What shall I do? (*Enter China on her way to the door.*) China, for Heaven's sake hide me some·where. I'll die if anybody comes. For goodness sake put me somewhere.

CHINA. Shaw, honey; don't you be frightened. You get behind dem curtains. (*Points to portier over dining room doors.*) I specs it's one of dem huckster men. Dey's all de time a ringing de front doah bell. Po' white trash; dey don't know no better. (*Fannie hides behind curtains and peeps through while China goes to the door, opens it, and discovers Clara.*)

CHINA. In de lan' of goodness, ef it aint Miss Clara. Why, howdy, honey.

FANNIE. (*In dismay.*) Merciful Heavens! It's Clara Boswell. I'm lost. (*Pulls curtains too.*)

CLARA. (*Coming in.*) Howdy do, China. Anybody at home?

CHINA. No, indeed, honey.

CLARA. Then I'll come in. I'm awfully scared. If mamma knew I was here, there would be a pretty howdy do at home. But, thank goodness, she's at the matinee. China can you keep a secret?

CHINA. Yass, indeedy.

CLARA. Well, I'm going to marry Mr. Jenkins very soon, and we are going to live here. We talked it over last night, and come to the conclusion to keep you, if you would like to stay. Now, remember, this is a secret, and if you value your place don't you mention it. There's a dollar for you. (*China courtesys.*) You needn't wait. I want to look around and see if anything is needed in the way of furnishing.

CHINA. Make yo'self at home, Miss Clara. (*Going.*) (*Aside.*) De lan' of goodness! If she finds Miss Fannie, dar'll be some ha'r pullin', suah. (*Exit.*)

CLARA. I'm afraid I have done a very unwise thing in telling China, but I had to give some reason for my being here. Now, let me see. (*Sits down and looks around room.*) I hardly like the way the furniture is arranged, but it wont take long to arrange it to suit myself when I come in as mistress of the house. I think the piano would look better over there. (*Designates a different place from the one Fannie pointed out.*) The pictures want to be rehung, and I think I'll have the curtains changed. Pale blue plush would look better. I think these are nothing but cotton velvet. (*Starts toward curtains, door bell rings. Clara very much startled.*) Good gracious! It can't be any of the young men. What shall I do? If they should come in and find me here I'd die. (*Enter China, going to the door.*) China, for mercy's sake hide-me somewhere. Oh, I'm frightened to death! Where can I hide?

CHINA. Don't kerry on so, chile; nobody's gwine to hurt you. I specs it's de chicken man. De never does ring de basement bell. You just step behind dat screen by de mantel, and I'll send him about his business mighty quick.

(*Clara hurries behind screen and peeps around it, while China goes to the door, which she opens, discovering Susie.*)

CHINA. For the lan's sake if it aint Miss Susie. Howdy, honey.

FANNIE. (*Peeping through the curtains.*) Susie Jones, by all that's wonderful. I'd give my best silk dress to be safely out of this. (*Closes curtains.*)

CLARA. (*Peeping from behind screen.*) Great goodness, it's Susie Jones, of all persons. (*Disappears behind screen.*)

SUSIE. You are sure that none of the young men are in?

CHINA. Deed I'se suah, honey. No young men about de place.

Susie. Well, I can't stay but a minute. I promised Charlie I'd drop in this afternoon and look around. I want to tell you a great secret, China, but you must cross your heart you wont tell.

China. Deed I will, but I specs I can guess it. You and Misto Charlie is gwine to get married and comin' up hyah to libe. (*Laughs.*) Yah, Yah, Yah. Aint dat it?

Susie. (*Surprised.*) Yes, but how in the world did you know it?

China. Oh, a little bird told me, sides yore old auntie aint bline.

Susie. Don't be a fool, China. Here's a dollar for you. You needn't wait. Mind you don't breathe a word about my having been here.

China. No indeedy, honey. Is you gwine to keep me when you and Misto Charlie come hyah to libe?

Susie. Yes, if you are a good girl.

China. (*Laughs.*) Yah, Yah, Yah. (*Exit.*)

Susie. (*Sitting in chair.*) Well, there would be a nice mess at home if papa knew I was here, but he's at the bank, and I'm supposed to be out shopping. (*Looks around.*) This is quite cosy, I declare. I'll make some changes in the—(*hears a noise at the door.*) Good gracious! that sounds like a latch key. It cant be the boys coming home from office. (*Very much frightened.*) It is. I must hide somewhere. O, if I'm caught, I'll never dare to look at them again. (*Runs behind second screen.*)

Fannie. (*Aside.*) This is awful. I feel fainty.

Clara. (*Peeping from behind screen. Aside.*) This is simply diabolical.

(*Enter* Herbert, Charlie *and* Rob *talking.*)

Herbert. Pious scheme, that, of closing office an hour earlier on Saturdays.

Rob. Yes, I wish every day were a Saturday.

Charlie. While you are wishing, wish every day were a Sunday, and then office would be closed all day. (*Goes to table and picks up letters.*) Here's the mail. Bennings, Singleton,

Bennings, Stacey, Singleton, Stacey. (*They take the letters and sit down to read them.*)

ROB. (*Opening letters.*) Hang it, a dun as usual. Shears & Co. want their little bill settled. I'll stop dealing with them. They are always wanting money. (*Throws bill on floor and proceeds to open second letter.*)

HERBERT. Here's one from the florist, $27. "Please remit." Yes, I will when I get good and ready. (*Tosses letter on floor and proceeds to open second letter.*)

CHARLIE. Well, mine aint a dun, but it might as well be. It's an invitation to a wedding. Sam Slocum and Hattie Fendall, and that means $25 for a present.

HERBERT. I'm in for it too. (*Holds up invitation.*)

ROB. So am I. Hang weddings anyway. What an idiot a man is to tie himself for life to some fool girl. Hattie's well enough in her way, but I for one, wouldn't marry the best girl on earth.

CHARLIE. (*Lighting cigarette.*) How about, Clara, my boy? I'm getting a little suspicious of you in that quarter.

ROB. Clara Boswell? Oh, she's a dear, innocent little thing, believes all I tell her—and—well, she's good enough to flirt with to pass time away.

CLARA. (*Peeping from behind screen.*) Oh! you wretch!

ROB. But how about you and Susie? It seems to me you spend most of your evenings there.

CHARLIE. Well, what if I do? It's no sign that I'm spoons on her. I like her well enough, but she's not my style. Good summer girl.

SUSIE. (*Aside, peeping from behind screen.*) A good summer girl; I'd like to scratch your eyes out.

ROB. I think Herbert here, is the shaky one. Twenty-five dollars worth of flowers in one month is going it rather strong.

HERBERT. (*Laughs.*) Yes, dear chappies, it costs money, these little flirtations, but we must have them you know.

CHARLIE. Then there is nothing serious between you and Fannie?

HERBERT. Serious! Well I should hope not. Fanny is a dear spoony little goose and it comes perfectly natural for a fellow to make love to her; but as for marrying her—why—I'd as soon think of marrying my grand mother.

FANNIE. (*Stepping from behind curtain.*) You would, would you?

HERBERT. (*Jumping up.*) Great Heavens, Fannie, you here. (Rob. & Charlie *whistle.*)

FANNIE. Yes, I'm here, and what's more I've heard every word you've said.

HERBERT. (*Starting towards her.*) But Fannie—

FANNIE. Don't touch me. Don't come near me. You mean, mean fellow. Clara Boswell and Susie Jones, you might as well come out from behind those screens. We are all in the same boat. (*Commences to cry.*)

(Clara *and* Susie *step from behind the screens.*

CHARLIE. Great Jupiter!

ROB. Holy smoke!

CHARLIE. How in the name of all that's curious, Susie, do you happen to be here at this hour. I told you to be sure and get away before three.

SUSIE. (*Witheringly.*) I know you did, *Mister* Stacey, but I'm very glad I stayed. A good summer girl am I?

CHARLIE. Oh come now, Susie, you know—

SUSIE. If you come near me I'll scream. (*Commences to cry.*)

CLARA. (*To* Rob.) Don't say another word to me, Mr. Bennings. I despise you. (*The three girls weep on each others shoulders. The three fellows look at each other in dismay.*)

HERBERT. Well, this is an awfully distressing scene and I'll put an end to it by making a confession. What I said about my feelings for Fannie is not true. She is just the dearest, sweetest little woman on earth, and I love her dearly; and what is more, we are to be married on the 30th of this month. We settled it last night. So you fellows might as well get ready to move.

ROB. Don't be so fast, my dear fellow, I fibbed about my

affair with Clara. We are engaged, and last night settled on the 29th, for *our* wedding, so I'm one day ahead of you, and it's you and Stacey, who will have to do the moving and not me.

HERBERT. The devil you say.

FANNIE. (*To* Clara.) You mean deceitful thing. (*Goes over to* Herbert.)

CHARLIE. (*Laughing.*) Well by Jove, this is rich. (*Aside.*) Now watch me kill them. (*Aloud.*) Boys, I guess you are in the soup. I overheard your little plans of last evening, and as all is fair in love and war, Susie and I fixed *our* wedding for the 28th. So I have you both. Sorry for you fellows, but such is the case.

HERBERT. I didn't think you capable of such duplicity.

ROB. Nor I. Your conduct has been shameful.

FANNIE. Susie Jones, I always did despise you.

CLARA. You are a bold shameless thing, and I've a good mind to scratch your eyes out. (*Goes to* Rob.)

(*Enter* Uncle Larry *and* Aunt Jane.)

UNCLE LARRY. Hello! Hello! What all this?

HERBERT. (*To* Uncle Larry.) Stacey here has treated us shamefully; he has been crying down matrimony and pretending he cares nothing for Susie Jones and he has just informed us that.—

ROB. (*To* Uncle Larry.) Why there's just the devil to pay. Stacey has been playing a double game with us and it turns out that he and Susie are to be married on the 28th and we have to get out.—

FANNIE. (*To* Aunt Jane.) Oh, Aunt Jane, it's just the meanest thing, you ever heard of. Susie Jones has deceived us in the most shameful manner. I just despise her and—

CLARA. (*To* Aunt Jane.) Miss Meredith, I'm glad you've come and I want you to take me home. We've just had an awful time and I'm just sick, and—and—heart broken.—

(*The above lines* of Herbert *and* Rob., Fannie *and* Clara *must all be spoken at once.*)

UNCLE LARRY. For goodness sake, one at a time.

AUNT JANE. I can't make out a word of what you are saying.

CHARLIE. Well, if you can keep the mob quiet for a few minutes, I will try and explain how things stand. There is no use of repeating to you the agreement we fellows entered into when Paradise Flats was started, for it was explained to you last night, that the first fellow who married fell heir to the house and furnishings. It seems that all three of us have been scheming, and each to get ahead of the other. I happen to be the successful one. Herbert and Fannie have announced their wedding for the 30th of this month. Rob and Clara went one better and announced theirs for the 29th, while Susie and I made up our minds last evening that we would be led out to slaughter on the 28th. Consequently, according to the terms of the agreement, the house and furnishings come to me, as my wedding will take place first. I feel a little conscience stricken in regard to you, but everything was explained to you last evening, and you professed yourself willing to take the chances. Besides these arrangement were made after we took you in. But the house is too large for Susie and me, and you shall come and live with us. Shan't he Susie.

SUSIE. Yes, indeed, Uncle Larry, and we'll make you so comfortable.

UNCLE LARRY. You are awfully kind, my dear children. Dear! Dear! It seems to me that I've been very cleverly taken in and done for. Are you not ashamed of yourself, you little scamps, to play such a confidence game on an old man like me?

HERBERT. You are not the only one buncoed. Look at me. They've regularly done me up.

ROB. And me, it's simply outrageous.

UNCLE LARRY. Why, hang your impudence, you young rascals, you are as bad as he is. You've tried to do each other up, and the smartest one has come out ahead. Why, I struck a regular nest of sharpers when I came to this house.

CHARLIE. Oh, come now, Mr. Singleton, that is putting it rather strong. We didn't invite you to come in with us. You, yourself proposed it and you should stand by your bargain.

UNCLE LARRY. (*Meaningly.*) I mean to, never fear.

CHARLIE. Well, then, the matter is settled, I hope.

UNCLE LARRY. Well, not quite. You see—(*Aside*) I'll break his heart—(*Aloud*) I think my young friend you are counting your chickens before they are hatched. What's to prevent me from getting married on the 27th.

CHARLIE. You. Oh, I say that wouldn't be fair, because you now know the dates we have fixed, and consequently you would be taking undue advantage of us by doing such a thing.

UNCLE LARRY. I didn't know them last night, did I?

CHARLIE. Certainly not.

UNCLE LARRY. Nor until a few minutes ago.

CHARLIE. No.

UNCLE LARRY. Well, I have a confession to make. Come here Jane. Young ladies and young gentlemen, permit me to present my wife.

ALL. What.

HERBERT. Why Uncle Larry, what does this mean?

FANNIE. Why Aunt Jane, what does this mean?

UNCLE LARRY. It means this, my young friends. Fifteen years ago a foolish quarrel separated two loving hearts. One was mine, the other Jane Meredith's Last night we met for the first time. Explanations followed. We found there had been a terrible mistake. Despite the lapse of time the old love flame burned as brightly as ever, and I determined that now, I had my sweetheart again, I'd take care not to lose her, and so we were married this afternoon. You youngsters may clear out as soon as possible.

HERBERT. Well, talk about taking a serpent to your bosom.

ROB. Or being buncoed.

CHARLIE. And taken in and done for.

FANNIE. Aunt Jane, I never would have believed you capable of such a thing.

CLARA. I'm glad of it.

SUSIE. And I have to give up this lovely little house. It's too bad. (*The girls surround* Aunt Jane.)

CHARLIE. Well, Uncle Larry, you've done us up nicely, but I for one bear no malice, and I congratulate you most heartily. (*Shakes hands.*)

ROB. And so do I. (*Shakes hands.*)

HERBERT. I guess I'll have to follow suit. (*Shakes hands.*) Well, fellows, I guess we'll have to go back to boarding and give up all thoughts of matrimony for a while, at least.

UNCLE LARRY. Well, well, this is rich. You all take my *coup de etat* so good naturedly, I can't find it in my heart to longer tease you. I have no idea of turning you out of your cozy little home. I'll tell you what I will do. Fortune has been kind to me, and I really have more money than I know what to do with. I'll tell you what, if you youngsters will have a triple wedding, I'll buy and furnish three houses exactly alike and give them to you as wedding presents. Come now, what say you? Is it a go?

HERBERT. Uncle Larry you are a brick. What say you Fannie.

FANNIE. I for one, say yes, and thank you heartily.

ROB and CHARLIE. (*Turning to Clara and Susie.*) What do you say girls?

CLARA. ⎫ Oh, we couldn't think of spoiling such a splen-
SUSIE. ⎭ did ending to a delightful romance.

UNCLE LARRY. Then it's agreed, so let the merry wedding bells prepare to ring, and may the serpent of discord and unhappiness never enter the portals of Paradise Flats.

CURTAIN.

CPSIA information can be obtained
at www.ICGtesting.com
Printed in the USA
LVHW061423071118
596180LV00020B/978/P